L.L. BEANIE WEENIE
GOURMET
IGUANA FOOD
FLOSS
SCUBA
WATCH
TICKET
FLT# 73
SEAT
31 A
KONO
PASTE
FLUORIDE-FREE
BOTTOM
TONE
SUN BLOCK
16 FL OZ
OF FLORIDA

I Wanna Go Home

KAREN KAUFMAN ORLOFF • DAVID CATROW

G. P. Putnam's Sons • An Imprint of Penguin Group (USA)

G. P. PUTNAM'S SONS
Published by the Penguin Group
Penguin Group (USA) LLC
375 Hudson Street
New York, NY 10014

USA | Canada | UK | Ireland | Australia
New Zealand | India | South Africa | China
penguin.com
A Penguin Random House Company

Library of Congress Cataloging-in-Publication Data
Orloff, Karen Kaufman. I wanna go home / Karen Kaufman Orloff ; illustrated by David Catrow. pages cm
Summary: Through a series of letters, Alex tries to convince his parents that he should not be staying with his grandparents while they are away, but slowly comes to realize that he can have fun, even at Happy Hills Retirement Community.
[1. Letters—Fiction. 2. Grandparents—Fiction. 3. Family life—Fiction. 4. Humorous stories.] I. Catrow, David, illustrator. II. Title.
PZ7.O6332Ig 2014 [E]—dc23 2013039319

Manufactured in China by South China Printing Co. Ltd.
ISBN 978-0-399-25407-9
1 3 5 7 9 10 8 6 4 2

Design by Annie Ericsson.
The illustrations were done in pencil, watercolor and ink.

For Grandma Shirley

and Grandpa Ralph—K.K.O.

TO HILLARY and MATT-

The Beginning—D.C.

Dear Alex, Ethan, and Annie,
We're so glad you are coming to visit us. You'll love it here! Do you know how to play bridge? It's a card game all our friends enjoy. When you come, we can play for hours and hours! Can't wait to see you.

Love,

Grandma Shirley
and Grandpa Ralph

P.S. Hope you like broccoli lasagna!

STONES TOUR
68

Dear Mom and Dad,

I know you want me to go to Grandma and Grandpa's house while you're in Bora Bora, but here's why I shouldn't. I'll have loads more fun at Stinky's. We're gonna play soccer, eat corn dogs, and sleep in the backyard with Lurch EVERY NIGHT! What could be better than that?

Love,

Boy Scout Alex

Dear Alex,

Your grandparents are really looking forward to having you all come. You can go to Stinky and Lurch's another time. Maybe.

Love,

Mom and Dad

P.S. Grandma says you can bring Iggy as long as he STAYS IN HIS TANK.

To: Mom+Dad@KidsMakeUsCrazy

From: Alex@IguanaBoy

Subject: Bored at G & G's

Dear Mom and Dad,

I'm at Happy Hills Retirement Community but I'm not happy at all! Grandma dresses Annie in girly outfits and treats her like a princess. Ethan found another annoying kid his age to play with. But I am bored, bored, bored! And did I mention it's raining? I WANNA GO HOME!

Signed,

Unhappy in Happy Hills

Dear Mom and Dad,

You won't believe this, but Grandpa doesn't have real teeth! He takes his fake ones out at night and puts them in a glass. They look like killer jellyfish.

When are you coming to pick me up?

Love,

Your nervous child, Alex

P.S. Please come get me. Hurry.

Dear Alex,

Bora Bora is very far away, so we can't come pick you up. But please try to have fun. Why don't you tell Grandma and Grandpa about your favorite things so they can get to know you better? In the meantime, here's a silly picture to cheer you up.

Love,

Mom and Dad

Dear Mom and Dad,

You were wrong! I took Iggy out to meet Grandma and Grandpa because he's my favorite thing, but Grandma screamed and Iggy got so scared he ran away. Grandma stayed on top of the picnic table for three hours. We finally found Iggy up a tree.

Grandpa says it's a good thing he didn't get eaten by an alligator. They live in swamps but sometimes they visit Happy Hills. I'm gonna go look for some now.

Love,

Swamp Boy Alex

DEAR ALEX,

STOP!!!! DON'T LOOK FOR ALLIGATORS!!!!

LOVE,

WORRIED IN BORA BORA

Dear Mom and Dad,

This will sound crazy, but Grandma and Grandpa don't have ANY video games on their computer or TV. By the way, they only have one TV. So when Grandma watches *The Young and the Breakfast*, Grandpa reads us stories about some guy named Peter Rabbit. Sometimes I wonder what goes on in the brains of old people.

Love,

Still-bored Alex

P.S. Tomorrow, Grandma is taking us to her square dancing class. I thought people her age didn't have to go to school.

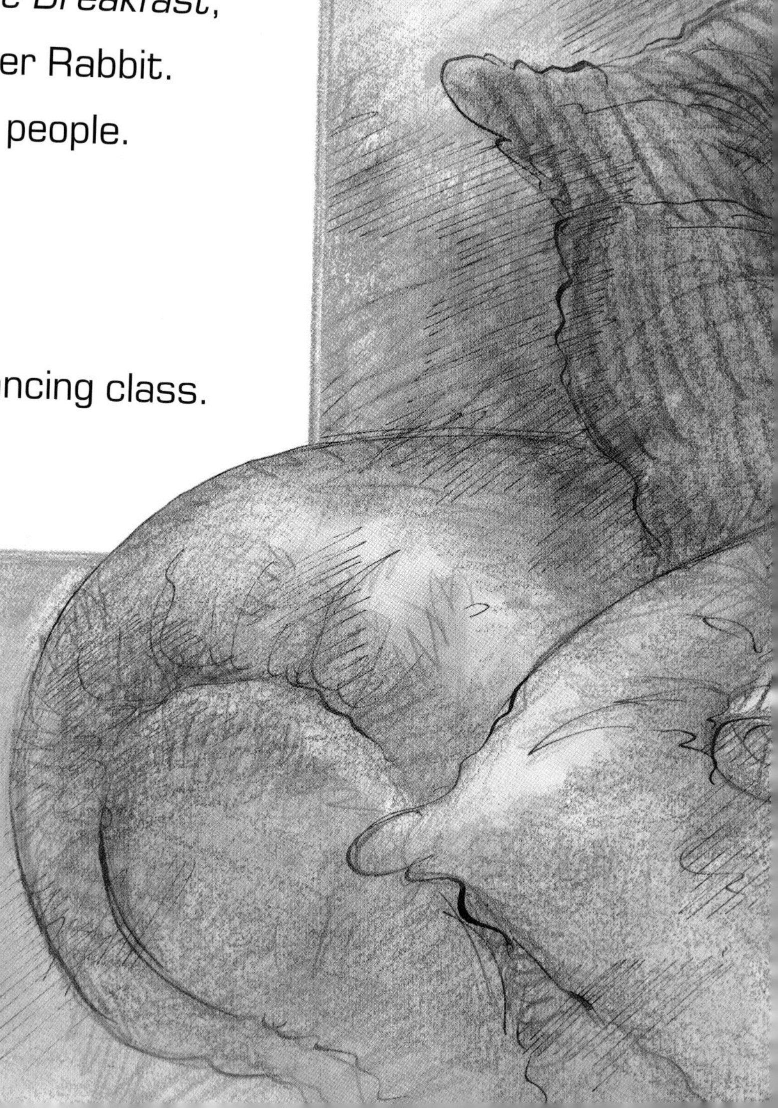

Dear Mom and Dad,

Did you know that when you go **square** dancing you actually spin in **circles**? I spun Annie around so much, she flew off my arm!

Love,

Your son who can really dance!

Dear Alex,

Please be careful with your baby sister. She's the only one you've got.

Love,

Your concerned parents

P.S. Tell G & G we will be home in a few days and to hang in there.

Dear Mom and Dad,

We played bingo at the clubhouse today and Grandma won. She got 13 dollars and 52 cents and gave it all to us to buy ice cream. Before dinner! Whoops, I wasn't supposed to tell you that. She said I could keep the change.

Love,

Moneybags Alex

SVEN
&
LARRY'S

Dear Mom and Dad,

It's raining again, but Grandpa borrowed a soccer ball and asked me to show him a few moves around the living room. He said soccer is almost as fun as stickball, whatever that is, and he didn't realize what he was missing all these years! And he's like a hundred or something.

Love,

Alex, the greatest soccer coach ever

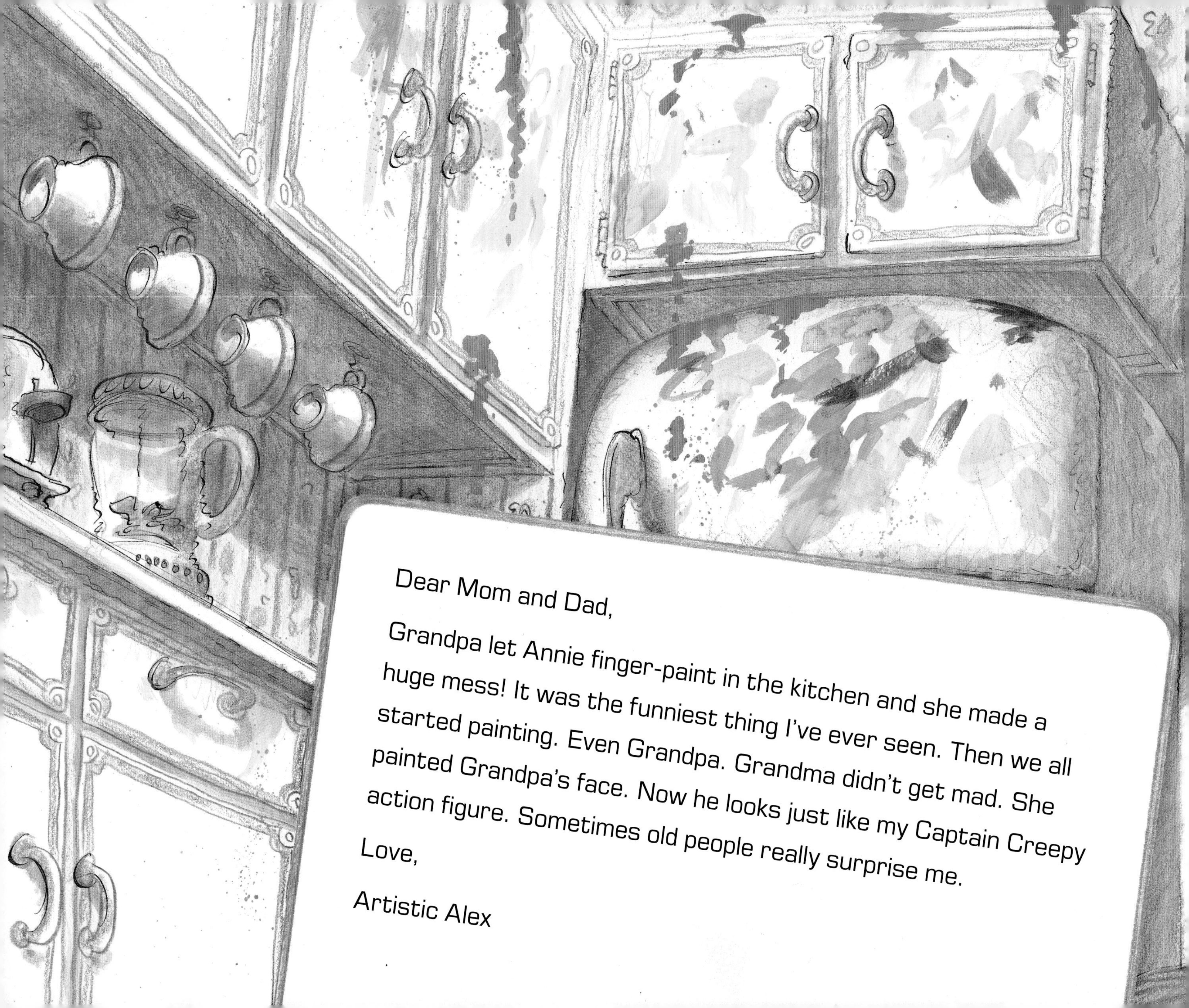

Dear Mom and Dad,

Grandpa let Annie finger-paint in the kitchen and she made a huge mess! It was the funniest thing I've ever seen. Then we all started painting. Even Grandpa. Grandma didn't get mad. She painted Grandpa's face. Now he looks just like my Captain Creepy action figure. Sometimes old people really surprise me.

Love,

Artistic Alex

DINER

Dear Mom and Dad,

We went to the early bird special at Moe's Diner and Grandma and Grandpa let us order whatever we wanted. Guess what I had? Corn dogs!

Hope you're having good food too!

Alex

16 EEEE

Dear Mom and Dad,

Grandpa said when he was a little boy, *his* grandpa read that same exact rabbit book to *him*! That's a really old book. And you know what else? He said he had a TV, but there were only five channels and they weren't even in color!

Could that be true?

Love,

Suspicious Alex

Dear Mom and Dad,

Me, Grandpa, and Ethan met Grandpa's friends in the parking lot for a stickball game. Grandpa taught us. It's a lot like baseball. You should see Grandpa hit. The ball almost broke Mr. Fletcher's window!

Love,

Your All-Star Hitter

"Are you sure you want to stay an extra week, Alex?"

"Yes! I wanna stay at
Grandma and Grandpa's . . .
please?"

Dear Grandma and Grandpa,
Thanks for a great two
weeks! See you next summer!
Love,
Alex

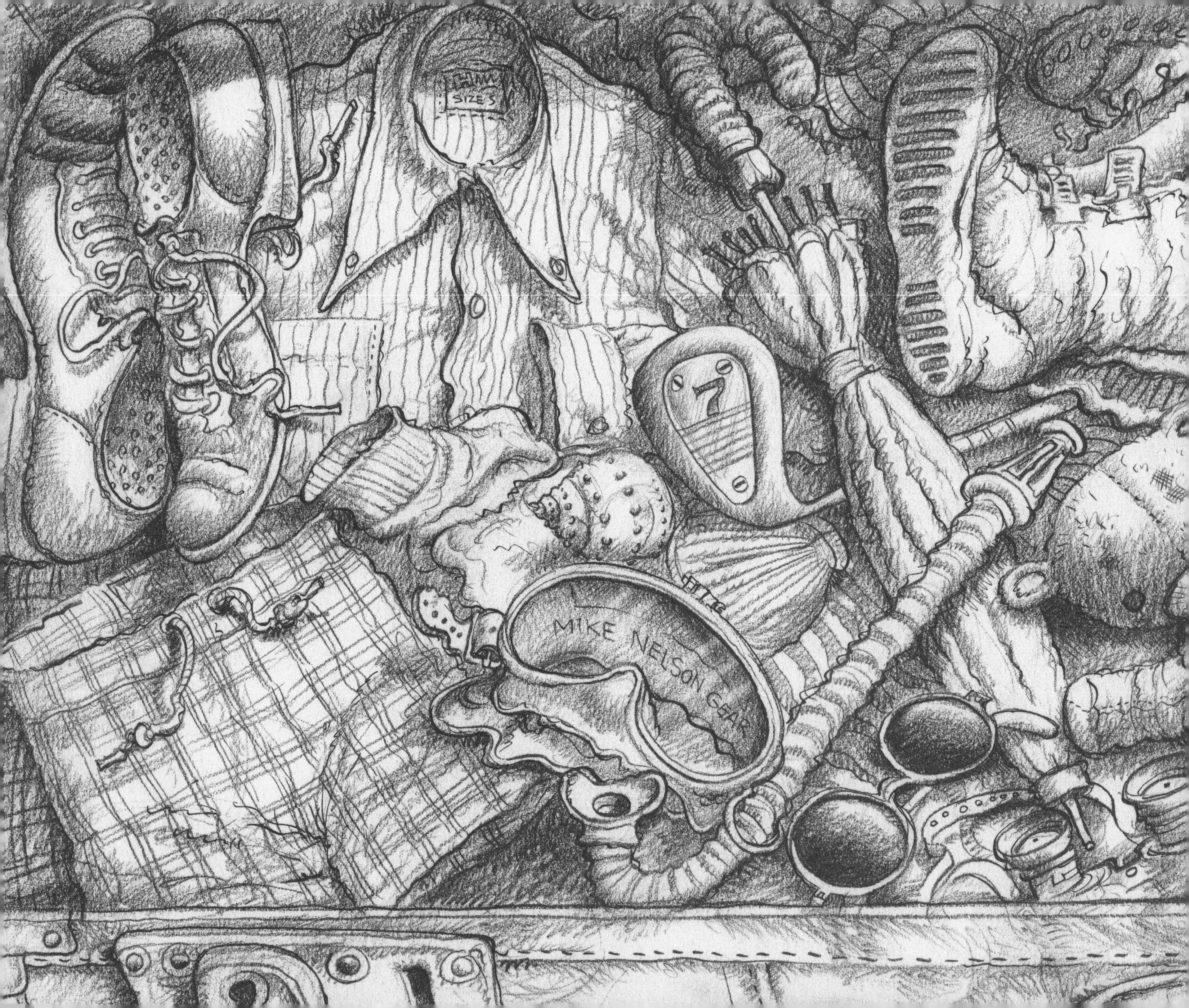
SIZE S
7
MIKE NELSON GEAR